UNICORN ACADEMY

Layla squashed her fear down and flung her arms around Dancer's neck. It seemed an impossible leap, but her instinct told her to put her faith in her unicorn. "I do trust you! I do!" she cried. "JUMP!"

LOOK OUT FOR MORE ADVENTURES AT

UNICORN ACADEMY

Sophia and Rainbow
Scarlett and Blaze
Ava and Star
Isabel and Cloud
Layla and Dancer
Olivia and Snowflake

★ ★ ★

UNICORN ACADEMY
Layla and Dancer

JULIE SYKES
illustrated by LUCY TRUMAN

A STEPPING STONE BOOK™
Random House 🏠 New York

To Emily French, who loves magic!

Text copyright © 2018 by Julie Sykes and Linda Chapman
Cover art and interior illustrations copyright © 2018 by Lucy Truman

Visit us on the Web! rhcbooks.com

Educators and librarians, for a variety of teaching tools, visit us at
RHTeachersLibrarians.com

Library of Congress Cataloging-in-Publication Data
Names: Sykes, Julie, author. | Truman, Lucy, illustrator.
Title: Layla and Dancer / Julie Sykes; illustrated by Lucy Truman.
Description: First American edition. | New York: Random House, 2018. |
Series: Unicorn Academy; 5 | "A Stepping Stone Book."
Summary: Layla must overcome her cautious nature and take her unicorn
Dancer on a dangerous ride to find a cure for the trees
dying around Sparkle Lake.
Identifiers: LCCN 2018041390 | ISBN 978-1-9848-5166-6 (trade) |
ISBN 978-1-9848-5168-0 (lib. bdg.) | ISBN 978-1-9848-5167-3 (ebook)
Subjects: | CYAC: Unicorns—Fiction. | Magic—Fiction. | Boarding schools—
Fiction. | Schools—Fiction.
Classification: LCC PZ7.S98325 Lay 2018 | DDC [Fic]—dc23

Printed in the United States of America
10 9 8 7 6 5 4 3 2
First American Edition

CHAPTER 1

The sun shone on the marble towers of Unicorn Academy as Layla ran to the stables. She couldn't wait to show her beautiful unicorn, Dancer, the new sparkly hoof polish that had arrived from her parents. She planned to brush his velvety coat and then paint his hooves.

Layla had loved unicorns for as long she could remember. It had been a dream come true when, just after her tenth birthday, she'd traveled with her parents across Unicorn Island to become a student at Unicorn Academy. On their first day at the academy, students were paired with their

very own unicorn. Each pair spent the next year working together and learning to trust each other so that they could bond and graduate to become guardians of Unicorn Island.

Layla had been delighted when Ms. Primrose, the wise head teacher, had paired her with Dancer. He was very handsome, and his snow-white coat had pink, yellow, and indigo patterns that matched the color of his mane and tail. But Layla loved him most for his kind, thoughtful nature. He was perfect!

I'm so lucky, she thought as she reached the stables. Being at Unicorn Academy was amazing. It wasn't just because she had a unicorn of her own; she also loved the lessons and, although she'd felt quite shy at first, she'd made friends with the five other girls in Sapphire dorm.

The stables' shiny automatic carts full of hay trundled down the aisle in front of her as she

walked in. Layla called out, "Good morning!" but there was no reply. The stalls that the Sapphire dorm unicorns slept in were empty. As it was such a lovely morning, Layla decided the unicorns must have gone out to play. She hurried back outside and found them gathered beside a rainbow-colored stream that ran through the meadow. All the streams and rivers in the land contained water that flowed from Sparkle Lake, the huge magical lake in the school grounds. The water was very important because it nourished the people and the land and strengthened the unicorns' magic.

Layla paused. All the Sapphire dorm unicorns—Dancer, Blaze, Rainbow, Star, Cloud, and Snowflake—were standing on one bank of the wide stream.

"I bet you can do it, Dancer!" said Rainbow, tossing his brightly colored mane.

"You're the best at jumping," said Star.

"Go, Dancer! Go!" chanted Blaze, stamping her front hooves, her fire magic making sparks fly into the air.

Each unicorn had their own magic power that they discovered while they were at the academy. Dancer still hadn't found his magic. Layla hoped it would be something like healing magic. It would be lovely to be able to make people well. She definitely wouldn't want him to have something scary like fire magic!

She watched as Dancer reared up on his hind legs. He balanced for a moment and then rushed forward. Galloping toward the stream, he leaped into the air, soaring across the water with the grace of an eagle. He landed safely on the far side of the bank, and the other unicorns all whinnied.

"You're so good at jumping!" called Cloud admiringly.

Dancer's eyes shone with the praise, and Layla's heart sank. Dancer was great at jumping and Layla knew how much he enjoyed it, but she hated galloping fast and jumping and avoided both at all costs.

"The rest of us will never be able to jump that far," said Star.

Rainbow's eyes sparkled. "Then I guess we'll have to use magic to get across!"

He tossed his mane, and multicolored light shone from the center of his forehead. It arched across the stream, forming a rainbow bridge. Rainbow anchored the light to the ground. Whinnying happily, the unicorns galloped across it and surrounded Dancer.

Layla hesitated and then, shoving the hoof polish into her pocket, headed back to school. She'd let Dancer have some fun with his friends. She could paint his hooves another time.

"Layla! Wait!"

There was the sound of hooves cantering up behind her. It was Dancer. "Were you looking for me?" He pushed his nose against her chest. She stroked him, happiness spiraling through her as she breathed in his sweet smell—a mixture of hay and sky berries.

"I was. I've got some new hoof polish, but you look like you're having fun." Layla hugged

him. "Go and finish your game. I can paint your hooves later."

"The game's finished. Did you see me jump the widest part of the stream?" He nuzzled her, and she took out the polish. "Gold and silver! That's fancy! Should we go to the stables and try it out?"

"I really don't mind if you want to stay here," said Layla.

"I'd rather be with you." Dancer's eyes met hers.

Layla smiled, and they walked back to the stables, her hand on his neck. Dancer was totally selfless and very loving. She just wished she could be a better friend to him—she knew he would love her to go galloping and jumping with him.

As her fingers played in his pink, yellow, and indigo mane, she wondered when they would bond. She would know when it happened because a lock of her hair would turn the same color as

his mane. If she was being honest, she was a bit surprised it hadn't happened already. Four of the six girls in her dorm had already bonded with their unicorns. But maybe it would happen when Dancer finally discovered his magic. A worrying thought crept into her brain—maybe he wouldn't discover his magic, and they wouldn't graduate at the end of the year.

Most students spent one year at the academy, but those who hadn't bonded with their unicorns or whose unicorns hadn't discovered their magic by the end of the first year stayed for longer. Layla wouldn't mind staying at the academy, but it would be strange if all her friends graduated and she didn't.

"Look, there's Ms. Primrose," said Dancer.

Layla followed his gaze. The head teacher was cantering her majestic unicorn, Sage, across the school grounds toward the gates. Sage's mane

and tail were flying out behind him, shining pure gold in the sunlight. It was rumored that he was related to the first unicorns who lived on Unicorn Island.

"I wonder where they're going," said Layla, seeing that Ms. Primrose was wearing a backpack. "I hope everything's okay."

Unease trickled down her spine. Sinister things

had been happening at the academy. First, Sparkle Lake had been polluted. Then a nasty spell had caused the lake to freeze. And Layla knew the teachers suspected that dark magic had caused the sky-berry bushes that grew near the school to die. Sky berries were essential for the unicorns' health, and the unicorns' magic had already begun to fade by the time Ava found new sky-berry bushes in the mountains. Then there'd been torrential rainfall that caused the lake to flood and almost shut the school down. Layla and her friends in Sapphire dorm had saved the lake each time, and Ms. Primrose had been very grateful. However, so far the culprit hadn't been caught. It was horrible to think of someone trying to harm the unicorns and the lake. Layla couldn't understand why anyone would do that.

"Layla! Watch out!" a voice snapped.

Layla jumped and stopped walking. She'd been

so deep in thought that she had almost bumped into Ms. Nettles, the Geography and Culture teacher. Ms. Nettles glared down her pointy nose at Layla, her sharp eyes angry behind her glasses.

"Walking along with your head in the clouds, Layla! That isn't like you."

"Sorry, Ms. Nettles."

"Just look where you're going in the future. Now, out of my way. Ms. Primrose has been called to an urgent meeting and left me in charge."

"Is the meeting about the bad things that have been happening here?" Layla knew from her parents' letters that everyone on Unicorn Island was beginning to worry.

Ms. Nettles frowned. "That's none of your concern. If you've nothing better to occupy your time, then I've some empty beetle cages that need cleaning."

"Sorry, Ms. Nettles, but I've got something really important to do," said Layla, hastily diving into the stables with Dancer.

Ms. Nettles collected beetles, and although Layla found all the animals and insects on the island interesting, she didn't want to clean out some smelly old cages. Luckily, Ms. Nettles didn't pursue her but strode off toward the school, stopping briefly to pat her unicorn, Thyme, on the way.

"So do you think Ms. Primrose's meeting does have something to do with all the things that have been going on?" asked Dancer.

"I don't know," said Layla. "Maybe something else bad has happened that only the teachers know about."

Dancer nuzzled her. "If that's the case, then we'll have to work together to try to protect the academy and the lake like we've done before."

Layla nodded. "Yes," she said firmly, feeling fear curl in her tummy at the thought. She really didn't like adventures but wanted to protect her school. Her brown eyes shone with determination. "We'll do whatever it takes."

CHAPTER 2

After chatting with Dancer and painting his hooves with the glittery hoof polish, Layla hurried back to the academy for lunch. Rainbows sparkled on the walls of the building, reflecting up from the lake, which shone brightly in the late-summer sunshine. Layla ran to the bathroom to wash her hands and found the rest of Sapphire dorm there.

"I think it's Ms. Nettles," Scarlett was saying.

"What's Ms. Nettles?" asked Layla.

"We were talking about the time someone used magic rain seeds to flood the lake," said Isabel.

"And I think it was Ms. Nettles. She's so mean," said Scarlett.

Isabel, Scarlett's best friend, nodded. "I bet she thought if she could get the academy closed, she'd get an extra-long vacation. She really doesn't like the students being here."

"Which is odd for a teacher," said Sophia thoughtfully.

"She is odd, though," said Olivia. "I mean, who collects *beetles* for a hobby?"

"Well, beetles are quite—" Layla broke off as her friends stared at her. She'd been going to say *interesting* but changed her mind. "Weird," she finished. "Do you *really* think Ms. Nettles is the person causing all the trouble?"

"I do," said Ava. "Remember how she was on the mountainside when there weren't any sky berries for the unicorns to eat and we were chased by the scary cloaked figure on a unicorn? It could

15

easily have been her, couldn't it, Sophia?" Ava rearranged the blue sprig of forget-me-nots she always wore in her dark hair.

Sophia nodded. "And when we were looking for berries, the plants were bewitched and grew into a thorny cage, trapping us in. Thyme, Ms. Nettles's unicorn, has plant magic, so he could have made that happen."

Ava nodded, her brown eyes serious.

"I remember her acting suspiciously by the lake just before it froze over," said Scarlett.

"Okay, don't all freak out," said Olivia. "But guess who I saw this morning, down by the lake, drinking some sort of potion from a tiny black bottle? Ms. Nettles! And after that she climbed a tree!"

They all stared.

"She was drinking a potion and climbing a tree?" echoed Sophia.

Olivia nodded.

16

"That is *definitely* weird," breathed Ava. "Why would she do those things?"

"Because she's up to no good, of course. We should tell Ms. Primrose," said Isabel.

"We can't," Layla put in. "Ms. Primrose just left. I saw her on Sage. She had a backpack with her, and it looked as if she was going to be away for a while."

"Who's in charge, then?" said Scarlett.

Layla gulped. "Ms. Nettles." Her tummy did a somersault. If the others were right and she was to blame for the bad magic, what would happen now that Ms. Primrose had gone away? Judging by her friends' faces, she could see they were thinking the same thing.

"This calls for action," said Isabel decisively. "I vote we keep a close eye on Ms. Nettles while Ms. Primrose is away. If she's up to no good, we'll get proof and tell the other teachers."

The others nodded. "We should catch her red-handed so people believe us," said Scarlett. She held up her hand. "Sapphire dorm will save the day!" she exclaimed as the others high-fived her.

At lunchtime, in the large dining room overlooking Sparkle Lake, the girls from Sapphire dorm sat together. Ms. Nettles, sitting alone at the teachers' table, gave the girls and boys in the dining room disapproving looks as they laughed and chatted.

Layla studied her as her friends talked. Could Ms. Nettles really be the culprit? She *was* very strict, and Layla knew the others didn't like her—particularly Isabel and Scarlett, who were always getting into trouble in her lessons—but actually, Ms. Nettles had never been horrible to her. Okay, she could be a bit snappy at times, especially when people messed around, but she was a good teacher, and her lessons taught them a lot about the land. Layla often visited the library, and she had seen Ms. Nettles in there, chatting with the librarian and taking out books. She rubbed her forehead. Ms. Nettles was stern and hardly ever

smiled, but was she bad? And why would she want to shut down the school? If that happened, she would lose her job—and her home.

It doesn't make sense, thought Layla, turning over the idea in her mind.

"So what do you think, Layla?" said Ava. "Are you looking forward to it too?"

"What?" Layla blinked.

"Our cross-country lesson after lunch, of course," said Scarlett, taking a huge bite of pizza. "For the first time we're going to get to use the advanced course. No more baby jumps for us!"

"Awesome," said Isabel. "The log jump is enormous. I can't wait to try it with Cloud."

"Have you seen the water jump? It's like a lake." Scarlett's eyes sparkled. "I know! Let's jump it together."

"Cool!" said Isabel.

Layla pushed her food away as her stomach

twisted into a tight knot. Did everyone have to jump the scary-sounding log jump? She hoped not. Cross-country was her not her strong suit. She hated doing even the smallest jumps on the beginner course. She couldn't bear the thought of having to jump higher. Maybe she could pretend to have a headache and ask to sit it out? No, she couldn't do that. She couldn't lie, and besides, Dancer loved jumping. She was amazed at how high he'd leaped when she'd seen him messing around in the meadow with his friends. It wouldn't be fair to him if she deliberately missed the lesson.

Olivia leaned over and whispered in Layla's ear, "Are you feeling all right?"

"I'm fine. You know I don't like jumping." Layla gulped. "Sorry, I'm just being silly."

"No, you're not." Olivia gave Layla's hand a friendly squeeze. "But don't worry. You won't get hurt even if you fall off."

Layla nodded. If anyone ever fell off their unicorn, the island magic formed a protective bubble around them and floated them down safely. But it wasn't the falling that worried her. The thought of galloping and jumping made Layla feel sick and wobbly.

"Dancer will look after you," said Olivia. "Just try to enjoy it."

Layla gulped. Enjoy it? Olivia had no idea!

That afternoon, as they all rode to the start of the cross-country course, Layla hummed to herself so she wouldn't hear Scarlett and Isabel playfully squabbling over who could jump the highest. Layla's stomach churned with nerves.

"Cross-country! Yippee!" said Dancer happily. "This will be fun!"

"Not for Layla," said a snide voice. Layla's

heart sank. It was Valentina de Silva, the meanest girl in school. Her rich parents were trustees, and Ms. Nettles was her aunt. Valentina rode up alongside Dancer on her beautiful but snooty unicorn, Golden Briar. "You're such a chicken, Layla." She made a squawking noise like a hen. "Scared of a few cross-country jumps."

Layla's cheeks flushed. She told herself to ignore Valentina, but her eyes grew hot with tears.

"Aw, is the little baby going to cry?" mocked Valentina.

"Go away!" said Layla through gritted teeth.

Valentina smirked. "You'll never be a guardian of the island if you can't jump."

"And you'll never be a guardian if you can't stop being mean!" said Dancer hotly. He put his ears back at Golden Briar and made a face. Golden Briar shied away, catching Valentina by surprise so that she fell onto his neck. Dancer stamped, and Golden Briar whinnied and raced away, with Valentina hanging on for dear life around his neck. The other riders laughed and pointed as Valentina struggled to pull herself upright.

"She's horrible." Dancer rubbed Layla's leg

with his nose. "Don't pay any attention to her. I think you're amazing."

Layla stroked him gratefully, but she couldn't help thinking about what Valentina had said. What if she was right and you couldn't become a guardian unless you could jump?

I've got to be braver, she thought anxiously.

The class gathered at the start of the cross-country course. "We'll walk around first so you can look at the jumps and check the takeoff and landing," said Ms. Tulip, their cross-country riding teacher. "Then you can try a few small practice fences before you set off."

Ms. Tulip led the way on her short unicorn, Rocket. Rocket had a crimson-and-purple mane and tail, with swirls of color that looked like exploding fireworks. She was small, but she was super-quick and she could jump really high.

Ms. Tulip showed the class how to approach the jumps, and Rocket leaped gracefully over them. Dancer snorted excitedly. Layla felt like she was going to be sick.

"Please can we start jumping now, Ms. Tulip? Pleeeeease?" begged Isabel.

"All right." Ms. Tulip smiled. "Go and do the practice fences, then we'll jump the course together."

"Which jump shall we start with?" asked Dancer eagerly as everyone cantered off.

"Can we just have a look at them first?" As the words left Layla's mouth, she felt like such a coward.

Dancer didn't complain as he patiently walked around the practice fences so Layla could look at each one. A huge cheer went up a few fences away, and seconds later the sweet, sugary smell of magic drifted to them on the breeze.

They cantered over to join the others. Everyone was clapping and cheering, the unicorns stamping their hooves.

"Lightning's found his magic!" said Ava as Layla rode up.

Billy and Lightning suddenly took off, moving so fast that their outline blurred as they sped into the woods. There was a whoosh of air that made Layla's hair blow over her shoulder and Dancer's mane fly up in her face. Billy and Lightning appeared behind them.

Billy's face was flushed with excitement. "Did you see us? Lightning's magic is speed. It works in short bursts. It's awesome! Lightning gallops so fast it feels like we're flying."

Lightning tossed his electric-blue-and-yellow mane.

Layla laughed. "I saw a blur. Was that really you?"

Billy nodded. "I wanted Lightning to have fire magic, but this is way cooler!"

Layla congratulated Billy and Lightning, secretly very glad that Lightning had this magical

28

power and not Dancer. Imagine if Dancer's power was speed. Disaster!

"Let's get going on the course!" cried Isabel, and she raced off to the start.

Dancer started after them eagerly. "Here we go, Layla!" he said, heading toward a jump.

"No, wait!" said Layla, grabbing his mane in panic. He stopped, bewildered. "I can't do it, Dancer!" she shouted. "I just can't!"

CHAPTER 3

"Layla, dear. Is everything all right?" Ms. Tulip said as she rode up.

Layla rubbed her nose, unable to speak in case she burst into a storm of tears. She felt like such a failure.

"You're not comfortable doing cross-country, are you?" said Ms. Tulip kindly. "Don't worry, jumping and galloping are useful skills, but they're not essential. Your knowledge of unicorns, their welfare and magical properties, is outstanding, Layla. If you keep working this hard, you're going to make an excellent guardian."

"Even if I don't want to jump?" asked Layla uncertainly.

Ms. Tulip smiled. "Even if you don't want to jump. Now, while the rest of the class go around the course, how about you go back to school and groom Dancer?"

"Thanks, Ms. Tulip," said Layla gratefully.

She heaved a sigh as she and Dancer rode back to school. She was relieved to escape the cross-country course and to know she could still be a guardian without jumping, but she felt guilty for not being brave enough to face her fears. To make things worse, Dancer was being totally lovely about it, not complaining once, even though he was missing out on the fun. As they rode past Sparkle Lake, the cheers of her friends drifted to her on the breeze. The leaves on the trees rustled and several swirled to the ground, one catching in Layla's long black hair.

"That's supposed to be lucky, catching a falling leaf," said Dancer.

"But it's too early for the leaves to be falling. Summer's not over yet."

A red-eyed fly with pink-and-turquoise wings buzzed past her nose. Layla swatted it away and was immediately  joined by two more. Layla squinted at them. The flies were unlike any she'd seen before, and even though they were pests, their glittery wings sparkled prettily in the sunlight.

Layla stopped to groom Dancer in the meadow in the shade of a tree. As she combed out his tail, she heard laughter and the clatter of hooves as her friends returned from the cross-country lesson. Layla didn't feel like having company. Dropping

a kiss on Dancer's nose, she said, "I'm going to go now. I'm sorry. I bet you wish you had a braver rider, someone like Scarlett or Isabel."

"I wouldn't swap you for anyone." Dancer's whiskers were tickly on Layla's face as he nuzzled her. "I don't mind about the jumping. I just wish you'd trust me. I'd make sure you were safe."

Layla bit her lip. "I know," she mumbled. "And I'm sorry. I'll try harder next time."

Layla wandered through the grounds, hardly noticing where she was going, just wanting to stay out of everyone's way, until a strange sight stopped her in her tracks. Ms. Nettles was kneeling on the grass, her nose to the ground and her bony bottom sticking in the air. It was almost enough to bring a smile to Layla's lips despite the way she was feeling.

"Um, Ms. Nettles?" she asked. "Are you okay?"

"Stop!" Ms. Nettles shrieked as Layla stepped

toward her. "You nearly squashed a berry beetle!"

Layla saw a small purple beetle with silver spots crawling slowly across the path, carrying a huge ripe strawberry.

"It must have a nest," breathed Layla. She remembered reading about the berry beetle in a book that Ava had lent her. "They're not like other beetles, are they? They look after their eggs until

the beetles have hatched and the babies are big enough to forage for food."

"That's right!" Ms. Nettles exclaimed. "I didn't know that you liked beetles, Layla."

"I like learning about everything on the island," said Layla. "Plants, animals, geography, and history. It's fun finding out about different things and how they depend on each other."

Ms. Nettles gave her a thoughtful look. "How very sensible of you. I enjoy reading and research too, and I find beetles particularly fascinating. They are hard-working and good at solving problems, and they help the environment in many ways."

Layla was surprised. Ms. Nettles's voice was full of passion. "Take the berry beetle," the teacher continued. "Not only does it care for its young, but it's a gardener too. In the spring, when the berries start to grow, the berry beetle brushes the

35

new fruit with its legs to stop it from getting berry mold."

"Wow! That wasn't in Ava's book," said Layla. "That's really clever."

Ms. Nettles flashed Layla a rare smile. "Beetles are just as magical as unicorns in their own way, and they teach us a valuable lesson—you don't have to be beautiful, clever, or rich to do great things. Hard work, bravery, and loyalty are equally good qualities." She studied Layla. "So why are you here? Shouldn't you be in the stables washing Dancer down after your cross-country lesson?"

Layla sighed deeply. "Ms. Tulip said I could leave early. I really don't like jumping. She said it doesn't matter and I can still be a guardian." Layla wound her hair around her hand.

Ms. Nettles's usually stern face took on an almost sympathetic look. "Ms. Tulip is right, my

dear. You don't have to like riding fast to care for Unicorn Island. I myself am not fond of galloping, and it is my belief that understanding the island is just as important as flashy magic and showmanship. Magic and knowledge complement each other, and Unicorn Island needs both in the same way that it needs different types of people to be guardians, people with a variety of abilities and skills. One day I think you will understand." Pulling a tissue from her pocket, Ms. Nettles sneezed violently and then checked her watch.

"Goodness, look at the time! I've got so much to do. First, though, I'd better take another dose of my hay fever tonic." Ms. Nettles reached into her pocket. "Well, isn't that great. I left it in my room. I shall see you back at school." She picked up her beetle bag and strode away, sneezing loudly.

Layla stared after her. Had she and the others

gotten Ms. Nettles wrong? Surely someone who cared for the island as much as she obviously did would never harm it?

But if it's not Ms. Nettles doing all these horrible things, then who can it be? thought Layla.

CHAPTER 4

When Layla got back to the dorm, Ava pulled her inside. "There you are! We were about to search the library. We thought you might have been buried by an avalanche of books."

"Or kidnapped by an evil villain who wanted to use your knowledge of the island," said Sophia.

Before Layla could tell the others about her encounter with Ms. Nettles, Olivia started speaking. "You'll never guess what Ms. Tulip told us after the lesson."

"This is *so* exciting!" burst out Scarlett.

"What is it?" said Layla.

"We're going camping!" whooped Isabel. "On Sunday we get to spend a whole night with our unicorns in a tent on the edge of the woods!"

"Our unicorns aren't sleeping in the tent with us, obviously," said Sophia.

"Shame," said Ava, and they both collapsed in a fit of giggles.

Layla did her best to smile, but it felt like the blood in her veins had turned to ice. A night outside in the dark with only a thin bit of canvas to protect her from who-knew-what and two whole days spent galloping around the countryside? It was her worst nightmare!

"Is . . . is everyone going?" she stammered.

"Yes! It's not required, but who wouldn't want to go? It's camping with unicorns!" Scarlett leaped onto her bed and began jumping up and down with excitement.

On her own bed, Isabel bounced next to her. "It's going to be amazing! I think we should go for a midnight walk! When the teachers fall asleep, let's sneak off on our own."

"Genius!" shrieked Scarlett, almost falling from the bed in excitement. "A midnight walk deep in the woods."

"But the woods are out-of-bounds." Layla's

41

voice came out raspy, so she cleared her throat and tried again. "Aren't the woods out-of-bounds?"

"Yes, but we're going to be allowed to camp at the edges," said Sophia.

Scarlett's eyes sparkled. "Which means it will be an awesome chance to go farther in! Who's going to come with us?"

The blue dormitory walls rang with the cheer of "Me!"

Only Layla stayed quiet. *I don't want to go,* she thought anxiously. *What if something happens in the night? What if something horrible comes out of the trees?*

"You are coming too, aren't you, Layla?" asked Olivia.

Layla hesitated as Ms. Nettles's voice came back to her. *"Understanding the island is just as important as flashy magic and showmanship."* Of course, that was the answer! She felt as if a weight had fallen from her shoulders. She didn't need to go camping to

become a good guardian. She could just go to the library.

"I think I'll stay here," she said. "I'd rather catch up on some reading."

"But we'll miss you!" said Ava.

"Won't you be lonely?" said Sophia.

Layla smiled at her friends. "Honestly, I'll be fine. Just make sure you tell me all about it when you get back!"

Olivia slipped her arm through Layla's, looking disappointed. "Are you sure?"

"Yes," said Layla firmly, feeling relieved that she wouldn't have to go. "I really am."

The next morning Layla was woken by a shout from Ava. "Look at the trees!"

Layla had to pinch herself to make sure that she wasn't still asleep as she looked out the window. Last night the trees had been green and vibrant,

but now the leaves had changed to autumn colors, and huge piles were scattered over the lawns. Many of them had blown into Sparkle Lake and were drifting on the surface like an orangey-brown carpet.

"This isn't right," said Ava, a frown creasing her face. "It's far too early for the leaves to fall. What's going on?"

"Look, some of the teachers are out there," said Layla, pointing. For a moment she saw a figure behind the other teachers moving deeper into the shadows of the trees. It looked like Ms. Primrose. She must be back! Relief rushed through her. If something strange was happening again, then they needed Ms. Primrose at the academy.

"Let's go and find out what's happening," said Ava.

Throwing on clothes, they all rushed outside.

As they ran to where the teachers were standing,

Layla heard a humming, buzzing sound. "What's that?"

"Flies!" gasped Sophia. Swarms of red-eyed flies with glittery turquoise-and-pink wings were covering the trees' branches.

"Flash flies," said Ava.

"One of the biggest pests in the land," said Ms. Nettles. She was peering up into the branches with Ms. Rosemary, Ms. Lavender, and Ms. Tulip.

"Where's Ms. Primrose?" asked Layla.

"Away, of course," said Ms. Nettles sharply.

Layla frowned. She must have been mistaken in thinking she'd seen the head teacher in the trees.

Ms. Nettles looked grimmer than ever. "These flies attack in a huge cloud, sucking the goodness out of the leaves until they wither and fall."

Ms. Rosemary looked anxious. "If the trees lose their leaves at this time of year, they will die. We have to get rid of these flies."

"Ava," said Ms. Nettles. "Go and fetch Star—we need her plant magic. Ask my unicorn, Thyme, to come along as well. If the leaves continue to fall at this rate, not only will the trees die, but the leaves will silt up the lake and the water will stagnate. And if that happens"—her voice rose dramatically—"the whole of Unicorn Island will be at risk!"

CHAPTER 5

Layla could hardly bear to watch the leaves falling into Sparkle Lake as the flash flies swarmed over the trees. She ran to the lake and began to fish fallen leaves from the water. It didn't take long for her friends to catch on, and soon they were all helping. It was an endless task. The wet leaves were as slippery as wriggly fish and almost impossible to grab. When Layla did manage to scoop some between her hands, they slid through her fingers as she put them on the bank.

A thundering of hooves announced the arrival of Ava riding back from the stables with Star and

Thyme. Other students had also seen what was happening and come outside.

"Stand back!" commanded Ms. Nettles.

Everyone shuffled back, clearing an area for Star and Thyme. They trotted to the nearest tree.

CRACK!

In unison, the unicorns struck the ground with their hooves. Purple, green, and gold sparks spiraled up, twisting around the branches of the trees. The branches shuddered.

CRACK!

More sparks, a rich sweet smell, and then tiny buds shot from the tips of the branches. The buds unfurled like fingers into fresh new leaves. A cheer rang up from the students.

CRACK! CRACK! Star and Thyme stamped their hooves repeatedly. Sparks flew, the trees made popping noises, and the air was heavy with the magical smell of burnt sugar.

Star and Thyme moved between the trees, stamping their hooves as they worked their magic in a crackling, popping shower of colored sparkles. Over the top of the noise came a volley of sneezes.

"Poor Ms. Nettles!" Layla thought the teacher was being very brave, sticking to Thyme's side even though the new leaves were playing havoc with her hay fever. Ms. Nettles's nose was red, and tears streamed from her eyes.

"The flies are multiplying!" exclaimed Olivia.

"They're ruining the new leaves." Layla watched in horror as a gigantic swarm of flies arrived in a glittering ball of turquoise and pink. Their red eyes flashed as they descended on the new leaves to suck out the goodness.

"Look at the lake," said Sophia.

The rainbow-colored water of Sparkle Lake was now a sorry sight, its surface covered in dead brown leaves.

Star and Thyme battled on, stamping their hooves, channeling their magic to grow new leaves faster and faster. Magic sparked and whizzed in the air, endlessly replacing the falling

leaves, until Ms. Nettles called for Star and Thyme to stop.

"It's no good," she told the unicorns. "If anything, the magic is making the situation worse by creating more leaves for the flash flies to feast on."

"We really need Ms. Primrose," said Jake, a dark-haired boy from Amber dorm.

"If only she was here," agreed Layla. "Oh, why did this happen just after she went away?"

Olivia let out a squeak, then clapped her hand over her mouth.

"Olivia dear, what is it?" asked Ms. Rosemary in concern.

"Errrm . . ." Olivia started to mumble, but she was saved from answering by Ms. Nettles.

"Everyone, back indoors immediately," she commanded. "There's nothing more to be done here. Go and get ready for breakfast while we

teachers try to come up with a plan."

"What's up, Olivia?" asked Sophia as they headed back to school.

Olivia glanced around. "Not now. Later."

As soon as they got back to the dorm, Olivia shut the door.

"So what is it?" Scarlett asked her.

"Don't you see?" said Olivia. "I bet Ms. Nettles caused the infestation of flash flies! She's obsessed with beetles, so why not flies? She waited until Ms. Primrose got called away and then somehow brought those flies here. I saw her climbing that tree yesterday. I bet she was planting a spell in it to attract them!"

"Yes," breathed Isabel. "It has to be more than a coincidence that they appeared just after Ms. Primrose left."

"I *knew* it was Ms. Nettles doing all the bad magic," said Scarlett triumphantly.

"Wait!" Layla's face burned as her friends turned toward her. "I really don't think it is Ms. Nettles. I spoke to her yesterday while you were all doing cross-country, and she really loves Unicorn Island. I don't think she would ever harm it."

"But look at the evidence," said Sophia.

"She's always around when things go wrong," said Isabel.

"And what about her climbing that tree yesterday?" said Scarlett. "Right before the flies appeared!"

"She could just have been looking for beetles," Layla said awkwardly, "And . . ." Her voice trailed off as she saw her friends' disbelieving faces.

"You can think what you like, Layla," said Isabel. "But I'm sure we're right."

While the others continued talking about it, Layla sank back on her bed, wishing she was better at arguing with people.

The bell rang, and Isabel jumped to her feet. "Breakfast! Good. I'm starving. We can talk more about this later. And maybe our unicorns will have some ideas too."

Layla hung back as the others hurried out. Olivia waited for her at the door.

"Are you okay?"

Layla bit her lip. "Yeah. I'm sure it isn't Ms. Nettles, though, Olivia. Didn't you see how upset she was over the trees?"

Olivia thought for a moment. "She could just be a good actress. You have to admit she does seem the most likely person."

"Mmm," said Layla, getting to her feet. "I guess so." But despite her words, in her heart she was sure her friends were wrong and Ms. Nettles was innocent. The question was, how was she going to prove it?

CHAPTER 6

After breakfast, the girls from Sapphire dorm decided to go on a picnic ride. Layla wanted to go with them but knew they would gallop, so she told them she wanted to go to the library instead.

"Are you sure you won't come?" said Olivia. "I don't mind just walking and trotting with you while the others go on ahead."

"Don't worry. You know I love the library," Layla said. "And I want to see what I can find out about flash flies."

Olivia grinned. "You're the biggest bookworm I've ever met. Okay, we'll see you later."

When Layla reached the library, she glanced out of the large window opposite its entrance. She could see the rest of Sapphire dorm setting off on their unicorns. They were all smiling and chatting, and she felt a sudden pang of loneliness. She did love the library, but she also loved being with her friends. It was a beautiful sunny day outside, just right to go exploring. It was all very well to tell herself she had to do some research, but a picnic ride might have been fun.

With a sigh she went into the library. She walked among the rows of books. "Entomology," she whispered, loving the way the word made the study of insects sound both wonderful and exotic. There were lots of books to choose from and a couple purely on flash flies. Layla selected the ones that looked most promising and went to sit on a purple cushion under the reading tree. But for once, the books she was reading failed to cast

their magic. Usually, no matter what she was reading, she quickly got sucked in, but today the words seemed to make no sense. Her eyes jumbled them up as she read. She kept thinking about her friends and what they were doing.

Then her thoughts turned to Dancer. He must be so lonely, being forced to stay behind when his friends had gone on an exciting adventure. She really should go and see him. Picking up the pile of books, Layla gave up reading and went to find her unicorn.

The stables were spookily quiet. Layla found Dancer in the meadow by the stream.

"Hello, Layla." Dancer nuzzled her hands. "What are you reading about this time?"

"Flash flies." Layla put the books down so she could give Dancer a hug. She smoothed his sunrise-colored mane and rubbed him behind the ears. "I'm sorry. Almost everyone's gone riding except for us. You must be angry with me."

Dancer snorted. "Angry? Of course I'm not angry. I was a bit lonely, but now that you're here, I'm happy again. Are you going to read outside?"

She nodded, and they walked down to the stream. Layla could see tiny fish flitting about in the sparkly, multicolored water. Dancer stood with his eyes half-closed in the shade of a tree, while Layla sat with her back to its trunk and began to flick through the books. One was thinner than the rest. It was mostly about ants. But Layla's eyes alighted on a chapter title. The

page, spotted with mildew, was covered with tiny printed writing:

How to Cure an Infestation of Flash Flies in Trees

The best way to stop an infestation of flash flies, without harming the environment further, is to use fire beetles. However, fire beetles are extremely rare. They prefer a warm habitat. They can be coaxed to leave their homes temporarily, especially for a flash-fly feast.

"Dancer!" exclaimed Layla, waving the book at him. "Fire beetles can solve the problem. We just need to find some."

They heard voices and whinnying. Layla turned and saw her friends heading toward her.

"Layla!" called Scarlett, waving.

"We've been looking for you everywhere!" said Olivia.

"You missed a great ride," said Isabel. "Billy and Jake came too. You should have seen the races we had. Billy kept winning until we banned Lightning from using his magic!"

"Billy is being really annoying. He won't stop going on about Lightning's awesome magic," said Scarlett, rolling her eyes.

"I like my magic more!" said Blaze, stamping her hoof and sending fiery sparks flying up into the air.

"Your magic is definitely the best!" said Scarlett, hugging Blaze, who looked very pleased.

"What have you been doing?" Olivia asked Layla.

"Reading," said Layla, nodding at the books. "And guess what? I've found out something really useful. Fire beetles can stop flash-fly infestations!"

Ava frowned. "But aren't fire beetles really rare?"

Layla nodded. "Yes, but I bet there's a book somewhere in the library that will tell us where we can find some. I'm going to look."

"Not now!" said Isabel. "You've done enough reading for today."

"Absolutely. We're going to cool down our unicorns with a water fight, and you're coming with us," said Scarlett.

Cloud whinnied. "Water fight! Yippee!" He stamped his hoof. Sparks flew into the air, and suddenly, water flew up from the nearby stream in a sparkling arc. It splashed down over Scarlett and Blaze. Scarlett squealed, and Blaze spluttered.

"Whoops, sorry, you two!" Cloud said, but his eyes glinted with fun, and he didn't look sorry at all.

Isabel giggled.

"This water fight is on!" cried Scarlett. She
turned Blaze and galloped back to the stables,
with Isabel, Olivia, and Sophia following.

"I'll come with you," Ava said, sliding off Star's back and joining Layla. "So what else did you find out about fire beetles?"

Ava and Layla walked back to the stables together. The others were waiting for them as they arrived, and they were hit from all directions by sopping sponges and blasts of water that Cloud directed from the water trough. Squealing and laughing, Ava and Layla grabbed sponges themselves and began chucking them back at the others.

After the water fight, there was no time to go to the library. The girls were all soaking wet. They showered and went down to the dining hall for supper, laughing and talking.

When they had finished eating, Ms. Rosemary organized a barn dance for all the students and their unicorns. A huge bonfire, lit by Blaze in a

whirling cloud of glittering red sparks, burned brightly at the lakeside, and its curling smoke kept most of the flash flies away. True to his name, Dancer was particularly good at barn dancing. Layla enjoyed trotting around in time to the jaunty music as she danced with her friends and their unicorns. However, she also watched Ms. Nettles, who was busy pulling mushy leaves from the lake and adding them to the fire to make it smoke. She was directing the other teachers to waft the smoke toward the trees.

"She's good," whispered Sophia. "No one would suspect her of anything bad!"

That's because she isn't bad! Layla wanted to shout.

Olivia appeared at Layla's side. "We're having a fire when we go camping tomorrow night. The second years said they got to toast marshmallows last year. Are you sure you won't come?"

Layla hesitated. Part of her wanted to go so

much, but in her head she just kept thinking, *Galloping . . . jumping . . . galloping . . . jumping . . . scary woods!*

"I'm . . . I'm sure," she said to Olivia.

Olivia sighed. "Okay, but it doesn't feel right when we do things without you. I like it when we're all together."

Olivia's words stayed with Layla for the rest of the evening and kept her awake that night. She remembered how much fun she'd had at the water fight and dancing and tried to find the courage to agree to go with her friends, but she just couldn't. All she could think about were the mysterious woods and the fast riding and all the scary things that might happen. No, it really was safer to stay home.

CHAPTER 7

The next morning, Layla waved her friends off on their camping trip and then headed for the library. On her way there, she paused by an open window overlooking Sparkle Lake. More leaves had fallen during the night, and the surface of the lake was now thick with rust-colored leaves. They even fluttered up from the fountain as it spouted water. A foul smell crept in on the breeze. The smell stuck in the back of Layla's throat, making her sneeze. *Poor Ms. Nettles,* she thought. *It must be even worse for her with her hay fever.*

Layla took out a notebook and listed all the

things she knew about fire beetles. They were shy, they feasted on flash flies, and they loved warm places. It wasn't much to go on. Maybe if she researched likely habitats . . . Layla skimmed through three books on deserts and two books on tropical climates without finding any reference to fire beetles. Then she saw a book on volcanoes.

Volcanoes! Of course! They were very warm places. There was a famous volcano on Unicorn Island: Mount Fury. Layla opened the book, and to her delight it contained several chapters on the volcano. She read fast, her eyes gobbling up the words until she found something:

While very few creatures can survive the heat of Mount Fury, there is one that positively seeks its warmth. The rare fire beetle prefers a home on the crater's edge, living there until the volcano erupts, when it will fly to safety.

Layla stared at the page. If fire beetles lived on Mount Fury, couldn't the teachers go there and bring some back? Layla quickly returned the book and headed for Ms. Nettles's study.

"Layla!" Ms. Nettles, who was half-hidden by a huge pile of books and papers on her desk, seemed irritated to see her. She sneezed. "I'm very busy. Please come back another time."

Part of Layla wanted to do as she was told, but she stood her ground. This was too important. "Ms. Nettles, did you know that fire beetles would chase the flash flies away? I found a book in the library that said they live on Mount Fury. Can't you go there and get some?"

Ms. Nettles frowned. "Oh, Layla, of course I know that fire beetles can help with flash flies. But Mount Fury could erupt at any time. It's far too dangerous to go there."

Layla felt suddenly hot, as a wild idea jumped into her head. She took a deep breath, wondering if she was completely crazy. "I'll go. Dancer will look after me."

Ms. Nettles's eyes softened slightly. "I know you want to help, Layla, but I will not have you and Dancer—or anyone else—putting yourselves in danger. I forbid it."

"But every day the lake looks worse!" exclaimed

70

Layla. "The fountain is clogged up, and the magic water can't flow around the island. Soon everyone will start to suffer, and if the water isn't cleaned up, the unicorns will get ill. We have to do something, Ms. Nettles!" She blushed as she finished and waited for Ms. Nettles to scold her, but the teacher just sighed.

"I'm sorry, Layla. Now please leave. I have lots to do."

Layla's head was in a whirl as she backed out of the study. She understood it would be risky to travel to the volcano. But the island was in danger. Should she stay safe and obey her teacher—or should she follow her heart?

Layla went to Dancer's stable. "Oh good," he said, looking very pleased to see her. "I'm so bored. What have you been up to?"

Layla quickly told him about her conversation

with Ms. Nettles. "I know she says it's too dangerous, but we need to find some fire beetles."

"Then let's go to Mount Fury—just you and me!" Dancer exclaimed.

Layla bit her lip. The cautious voice in her head was saying "No, no, no!" but deep down it felt like the right thing to do. They had to try to save the island.

"We could do it, Layla," said Dancer eagerly. "We could use the magical map to get there."

There was a model of Unicorn Island in the Great Hall that could take you anywhere on the island, although it was strictly forbidden to use the map without Ms. Primrose's permission.

"We'd be in so much trouble, and we won't have any of the others with us to help," said Layla slowly, but even as she spoke, her mind was made up. "But I don't care!" she declared. "We have to try to help!"

Layla and Dancer hurried into the school. Before they entered the hall, Layla crept into Ms. Nettles's classroom to raid the teacher's cupboard. There were several beetle bags hanging up on the back of the door. Remembering she was hunting for fire beetles, Layla chose the thickest bag and hung it over her shoulder. She returned to Dancer, and they went into the hall.

It was a huge room with a domed glass roof. The swirls of color in the glass filled the hall with rainbow light. On the walls were massive paintings of unicorns, and in the center of the room was the magical map —a model of the island in miniature, showing jagged mountains, lush meadows, and sandy beaches, with Unicorn Academy's glass-and-marble building right at its center, beside Sparkle Lake. Usually the lake shone, but today it was clogged with minuscule

leaves, and a brown cloud seemed to hang over the academy's buildings.

A magical force field of golden light surrounded the map. It buzzed and hummed. Layla's heart thudded as they approached it. She'd used the map twice before. Would the force field let her pass this time? Layla squared her shoulders and tried to look confident even though her insides were churning with doubt. She stepped into the light, and it dissolved in a shower of sparks. Layla's breath rushed out, and she grinned. If the map approved of her trip, then maybe this really was the right thing to do.

Dancer nuzzled her. "When we get to the volcano, we might have to do lots of galloping and jumping," he said, his voice serious. "Trust me, Layla. I'll look after you."

Layla met his eyes. "I know you will," she said. And in that moment, she really did know it. "And

I'll look after you too," she told him softly. "I promise." He nuzzled her and, with one hand on his mane, she took a deep breath.

"We need to find a fire beetle," she told the map, hoping it might help if the map knew what they were planning. She stretched her hand out and touched the rocky slope of Mount Fury. Colorful lights burst around her, and a fierce wind came from nowhere, plucking at Layla's clothes. She and Dancer started to spin around, twirling faster and faster, until suddenly they were falling. . . .

CHAPTER 8

Dancer plunged like a falling stone and landed with a bone-jolting thud. In a daze, Layla stared around. They were on the lower slopes of Mount Fury. High above them, the mouth of the volcano was belching out clouds of thick smoke. Something was tickling her neck. Layla swatted at it. Her fingers touched cold glass and marble. Caught in her hair was a tiny model of Unicorn Academy. Layla tucked the tiny building in her pocket. She knew from her previous adventures that she and Dancer would need it to return to the school.

"Phaaaarrw!" coughed Dancer. "It smells terrible!"

Layla looked up to the top of the mountain again, shielding her eyes. Fiery-red dollops of lava were spurting over the edge of the crater, and a pungent smell of rotten eggs drifted toward her.

"It looks like it might be about to erupt," said Layla anxiously. "We'd better find some fire beetles before it does. They live at the very top by the crater." She scrambled onto Dancer's back.

"Hold tight!" Dancer set off up the side of the mountain, his hooves scattering lumps of rock, sending them tumbling behind in a stony river. Layla's heart thudded painfully against her chest as his hooves slipped and slid on the steep, uneven surface. She gripped his mane until her knuckles whitened. She really didn't want to climb the volcano, but no matter how scared she was, she

wouldn't give up. If there were fire beetles on the volcano, she and Dancer would find them!

"Keep going, Dancer!" she urged.

He launched into a canter. "We'll soon be at the top," he panted. "We'll soon find those—" He broke off with an alarmed whinny as the ground began to shake. Layla squeaked in horror as a crack zigzagged across the rocky landscape, widening into a deep crevasse. She clung to

Dancer's mane, hardly daring to breathe as they teetered on the edge.

Slowly, Dancer crept back from the sheer drop, stones rattling under his hooves.

"That was close!" he gasped when they were safe.

"If we'd fallen in, we would have died!" Layla stared at the gaping drop in front of them. It was at least six feet wide, and she couldn't even see the bottom. "How will we get to the top of the volcano now?"

"We'll have to jump," said Dancer. "Trust me, Layla, I know I can clear it. I've easily jumped that far before."

But not taking off on steep, uneven ground, Layla wanted to say. What if there was another earthquake when he took off? What if the crack widened farther as he jumped? Would they fall into the hole?

Dancer sensed her worry and nuzzled her leg. "Layla, I can do this."

Layla's heart pounded, but they didn't have another option. "I trust you," she said finally. She gripped Dancer's sides with her knees and wrapped her fingers in his mane. Dancer took a few paces back, then cantered forward. Layla shut her eyes and felt him leap into the air. There was a moment when they were hanging over the crack, and then she felt his hooves thud into the ground as he landed on the other side. The breath rushed out of her. "You did it!" she cried, hugging him.

Dancer whinnied. "I did! Now let's get to the top as fast as we can!"

The nearer they cantered to the top of the volcano, the hotter it was. Dancer's sides soon grew slippery with sweat, and Layla felt a trickle run down her nose. It was hard to breathe.

"Almost there," wheezed Dancer.

"What's that?" Layla pointed to some tiny red spots on the rocks in front of them. "Are they fire beetles?"

"I don't know," said Dancer. He went closer and snorted in shock. "No! That's drops of lava!"

Despite the intense heat, Layla felt a chill seep through her. "The lava must be rising through the rocks. I read that happens just before a volcano erupts!"

"Maybe we should go back," said Dancer anxiously.

"But we're almost there! We have to go on," Layla insisted, looking up to the top.

"What if the volcano erupts?" asked Dancer.

"We'll have to risk it!" said Layla.

Thick smoke billowed toward them as they scrambled up the final steep slope to approach

the crater. Layla scanned the ground, searching desperately for fire beetles.

"There aren't any fire beetles here," said Dancer, reaching the crater's edge.

Just inside the crater, Layla could see an oozing lake of burning lava that hissed and spat, spraying fiery globs into the air. Layla's eyes were streaming. Where were the fire beetles?

"We should go," said Dancer as lava shot past his nose.

"Wait!" Layla caught movement in the corner of her eye. She slid from Dancer's back.

"Layla, what are you doing? Be careful!" whinnied Dancer.

"Shhh," she whispered, crouching down and pointing to a chunk of rock. Behind it were four very strange-looking beetles. Her heart leaped. "Fire beetles!" she whispered excitedly, recognizing them from the book.

The fire beetles were creepy, with spindly legs, thick black shells, tiny heads, and large pincers.

"Catch them!" urged Dancer.

As Layla steeled herself to pick them up, their shells opened, revealing acid-yellow wings that shimmered as they vibrated.

"They're going to fly away!" said Dancer. "They must know the volcano is about to erupt!"

There was no time to be squeamish. Layla tugged Ms. Nettles's beetle bag from her shoulder and opened it. She angled it over the beetles, ready to scoop them inside, but the beetles looked up and flew straight in.

"Great!"

"Layla, we have to leave. Jump on my back, quick!" said Dancer urgently.

There was a deep rumbling sound, and smoke erupted from the volcano, flinging molten lava everywhere. The ground vibrated more and more violently until Dancer could barely stand. Layla scrambled onto his back. The volcano was erupting!

"Go, NOW!" she shrieked.

BANG! The explosion almost blew Layla and Dancer over. Layla clung to her unicorn's mane, gripping his sides with her knees as he galloped away from the crater, leaping from rock to rock to avoid the boiling lava that was now flooding out of the crater and down the mountainside. It seemed to be chasing them like a fiery monster.

"Faster!" cried Layla. Forgetting all about her fear of galloping, she urged Dancer on, shouting at the top of her lungs. Dancer raced on, out-galloping the lava behind them. Hope surged

through Layla. If they could just reach some safe ground, then she could take out the miniature model of the school and use it to get home. . . .

"No!" she cried in horror as she suddenly realized that in front of them, two rivers of lava had curled inward, flowing until they met in the middle to form a giant lake right across their path. "Stop!" screamed Layla, terrified that Dancer would plunge straight into it.

"We can't!" cried Dancer. He headed for the lava lake at breakneck speed.

Layla felt a bolt of terror. He was going to jump! "Dancer, NO!" she yelled. No way could he leap something so big! He was great at jumping, but this was impossible. They would fall in and be burned to pieces!

"Trust me!" he whinnied. "Please!"

Layla squashed her fear down and flung

her arms around Dancer's neck. It seemed an impossible leap, but her instinct told her to put her faith in her unicorn. If he thought he could do it, then she had to believe him. "I do trust you! I do!" she cried. "JUMP!"

CHAPTER 9

As Dancer leaped into the air, Layla saw pinky-blue sparks and smelled something sweet. Magic! She felt something strange happening to Dancer's sides as he suddenly soared high in the sky! Layla had never felt so weightless, so exhilarated. The jump seemed to go on and on and she screamed at the top of her voice, "Wow! I love jumping!"

"FLYING!" Dancer's voice was full of shock and wonder. "I'm not jumping. I'm flying, Layla!"

Looking down in surprise, Layla realized that the strange movement she'd felt on his sides were huge feathery wings. The indigo wings, marbled

with pinks and yellows, had grown out from his sides and were propelling them upward.

"I've found my magic!" cried Dancer. "I can fly!"

Layla couldn't help herself. A whoop of sheer delight burst from her as they soared up into the sky above the smoke and into the clouds. She didn't feel scared at all. She was on her unicorn, and he was flying! This was the most amazing moment of her life!

Layla hugged Dancer tight. She trusted him completely and felt all his love and trust flowing right back at her. It was the best feeling ever.

Beneath them, fluffy white clouds floated by, and beneath that, through the smoke, she could just pick out a thick red line of lava rolling down the mountainside. They had the fire beetles and they were safe. Dancer flew on until they were away from the lava, and then he swooped down

in a graceful curve. When he landed, Layla half jumped, half fell from his back and hugged him again. "That was incredible!"

"Hardly any unicorns can fly!" Dancer said in astonishment. "I can't believe I can. I—" He broke off and nudged Layla, catching her hair on his nose and tossing it over her arm. "We've bonded! Look, Layla, we've finally bonded!"

Layla's heart swelled as she looked at the pink, yellow, and indigo streak now running through her hair. "I love you, Dancer!" She felt stronger and more confident than she had ever felt in her life. "Now let's get back," she declared. "We have some trees and a lake to save!"

There was no need to use the tiny model of Unicorn Academy to return to the school. Dancer just flew! He was so good at it, flying steady and fast as if he'd been doing it all his life. They soared away

from the volcano, heading over deserted tundra and then over thick forests and grassy meadows. Finally, the academy came into sight. Approaching Sparkle Lake, Layla saw two figures talking on its banks. "Look, it's Ms. Nettles, and there's Ms. Primrose with her!" she said to Dancer in surprise. "When did she get back?"

Ms. Primrose's voice floated toward them, loud and angry. "I came straight back when I heard there was a problem. Frankly, I'm disappointed that you didn't tell me about it sooner, Ms. Nettles. We must close the school immediately. The students cannot go on living here with this foul smell, and the damage the flash flies have caused to the trees could leave them unstable, liable to fall at any time."

"No, Ms. Primrose! It's okay!" cried Layla as Dancer flew down. "The school doesn't have to close."

"Layla! What is the meaning of this?" demanded Ms. Primrose. She blinked. "Dancer can fly!"

"Yes, he's found his magic, and we've bonded, but right now it's the trees that matter. We can save them. Look!" said Layla.

She pulled the bag off her shoulder and saw a look of hope light up Ms. Nettles's pointed face. "Layla, you didn't go to—"

"I did," interrupted Layla. "I'm sorry I disobeyed you, and I'm sorry I used the map without asking, but I had to help. I went to Mount Fury and found four fire beetles!"

"Oh, Layla, well done!" Ms. Nettles's glasses jumped on her nose as she clasped her hands together. "With four beetles we can definitely save the trees."

"And afterward you'll have four fire beetles for your beetle collection." Layla grinned at her. "Should Dancer and I fly up and put the beetles

in the trees?" She turned to Ms. Primrose and was surprised to see that, instead of smiling, the head teacher was frowning.

"It was very clever of you to find fire beetles, Layla," she said, her mouth tight, "but I'm really not sure they will help."

"They will," said Ms. Nettles.

Ms. Primrose shook her head. "No, no. I think it might be better if we keep them in a cage overnight while we do some research to check they won't damage the trees further. Give them to me, please, Layla."

"But I've done the research, Ms. Primrose," argued Layla. "The book I read said fire beetles are excellent at getting rid of flash flies."

"Layla's right," said Ms. Nettles earnestly. "Fire beetles will not damage the trees."

"I really don't think we should risk it," said Ms. Primrose. "Please hand the beetles over, Layla."

Layla glanced between the two—old, wise Ms. Primrose and passionate, knowledgeable Ms. Nettles. Who should she listen to? Instinct told her that Ms. Nettles was right, and her adventure had taught her to listen to her instincts. "I'm sorry, but I really think we should put the beetles in the trees, Ms. Primrose," she said. "And as soon as possible. Come on, Dancer!"

Dancer needed no encouragement. He flew up. Layla heard Ms. Primrose make a sharp noise, but she ignored her. She was absolutely sure she was doing the right thing. Dancer hovered above the top branches of the trees while Layla opened the beetle bag and let the fire beetles crawl out. One at a time, she placed them into the branches.

"Get rid of the flies," she whispered. *"Please!"*

The beetles split up and

scurried toward the flash flies. They started to gobble them all up. The flash flies began to panic. Their wings whirred. As the beetles stormed through the branches, the flies rose into the air, swirling together in a buzzing mass. The beetles reared up, waving their front legs at them and snapping their pincers. The flies set off across the sky, leaving the trees—and the academy—for good.

Dancer flew back to the ground and tossed his mane proudly.

"It worked!" said Layla.

Ms. Primrose smiled. "Excellent! Well done, my dear." Layla noticed her smile was slightly tighter than usual. She was sure it was because she had disobeyed her. Still, she knew it had been the right thing to do—it had worked!

Ms. Nettles looked delighted. "Well, I don't think we need to send the students home now.

Frankly, I think the academy is safer when they're here, especially the girls from Sapphire dorm!" Her lips twitched and she actually smiled— properly smiled—for once. "Now that the flies have gone, we can make sure the fallen leaves are cleared from the lake."

Layla heaved a happy sigh. The school could stay open, and soon the unicorns would have fresh, clean water to drink again so their magic would stay strong. Nothing else mattered as much as that.

"One more thing," Layla remembered. "This appeared when I used the map, but I didn't need it to get home."

She held out the tiny model of Unicorn Academy. Ms. Nettles went to take it, but Ms. Primrose got there first. "Thank you, Layla dear," she said, her hand closing tightly around it. "I'll

take care of that." She turned to Ms. Nettles. "Come with me, Ms. Nettles. We should talk about these attacks on the school. They cannot be allowed to continue. Layla, why don't you take Dancer to the stables?"

Layla nodded and watched as the two teachers hurried away. She stroked Dancer's neck, her initial relief and happiness fading slightly. It felt strange standing there, just her and Dancer. She found herself wishing that all her friends and their unicorns were there so they could celebrate together.

Dancer nuzzled her. "Are you okay?" he asked.

"Mmm." Layla sighed. "I'm really glad the trees are going to be all right, but I miss the others. I wish we could tell them about it."

"Well, why don't we?" said Dancer. "We could go to the woods and find where they are camping.

We don't have to stay overnight. We can just go for a few hours."

Layla hesitated. She loved the idea of going to see the others, but she didn't want to go if Dancer needed to rest. "Are you sure? You've done so much today already."

"I'm fine!" said Dancer, tossing his mane. "Flying makes me feel great! Shall we, Layla?"

She grinned. "Yes!"

CHAPTER 10

Layla got on Dancer's back, and he flew into the sky. He headed across the school grounds toward the woods. "We should be able to see their tent easily from up here," he said.

"We don't need to find their tent," said Layla. "Look, I can see them!" She had spotted the rest of Sapphire dorm and their unicorns standing at the edge of the woods. *What are they doing?* she wondered.

Dancer flew toward them. As he got closer, Layla saw Rainbow stamp one of his front hooves on the ground. Multicolored lights suddenly

illuminated a path through the trees.

"Hello!" Layla shouted to her friends, buzzing with excitement. What would her friends say when they saw Dancer flying?

"Was that Layla?" Isabel said in surprise.

Sophia was the first one to spot Dancer. Her mouth fell open. "Layla!" she squeaked. "Look up there, everyone!"

The other unicorns all whinnied in amazement as Dancer flew lower.

Scarlett's eyes turned the size of saucers. "Oh my . . . Wow!" she breathed.

"Dancer's got flying magic!" exclaimed Olivia.

"And you've bonded," cried Ava, pointing at Layla's hair.

"How did it happen? When?" demanded Isabel.

Dancer landed, and Layla got off his back. Everyone crowded around asking questions, and Layla and Dancer told them everything that had happened since they'd left school to go camping.

"Sounds like we missed a really awesome adventure," said Sophia when Layla had finished.

Ava hugged Layla. "You've been so brave. It was amazing that you went to the volcano all on your own."

Layla grinned. "I wasn't on my own—I had Dancer!" He nuzzled her hair. "So, what are you

doing?" asked Layla, looking curiously at the path of lights.

The others exchanged looks. "Um . . . we were planning a surprise for you," said Scarlett.

"For me?" said Layla in surprise.

Olivia linked arms with her. "We were missing you, and we were planning to go back to school and see if we could convince you to come here with us."

"We've done all sorts of things to try to make the woods less scary!" said Ava.

"Come and see what we've done for you!" said Isabel, pulling her over to the lights. "Start here on this path of light that Rainbow made."

Layla glanced around at her friends' eager faces, and her heart filled with happiness. Sapphire dorm was the best!

Putting her hand on Dancer's neck, she walked with him down the path of twinkling rainbow

lights, with her friends following. After a little way, the lights changed to small blazing fires.

"I made these!" said Blaze proudly. "They're magic so they won't burn anything they shouldn't."

The fires led back to a clearing on the edge of the woods, where there was a large pale blue tent with a bright blue flag. A campfire was burning outside the tent, and a pot of gently bubbling hot chocolate was warming above it. A rainbow arched over the tent, and all around it bloomed jasmine bushes, the tiny white flowers giving off a sweet, heady scent.

"Star magicked up those flowers," said Ava proudly.

"They're beautiful," said Layla, breathing in deeply.

"So, will you stay the night with us?" begged Olivia. "We've got a spare sleeping bag and pillow for you."

Layla beamed at all her friends. Her fear of camping by the woods had vanished now—if she could climb a volcano to do what she felt was right, she could do anything! "Of course I'll stay!" she said.

As the sun set and darkness fell, the unicorns munched on fresh sky berries from a sky-berry bush that Star had grown, while the girls cuddled up in their sleeping bags around the fire, dipping strawberries and marshmallows on sticks into their hot chocolate. Layla didn't think she had ever felt happier. She glanced across to the unicorns. As if sensing her gaze, Dancer lifted his head, and their eyes met.

Layla went over to him.

"Do you like adventures now?" he asked her softly.

"Oh yes." She breathed. "Especially when I'm with you."

She wrapped her arms around him and hugged him tightly, as high above them the crescent moon shone and the stars twinkled brightly in the sky.

Someone is trying to ruin
the graduation ball!
Can Olivia and Snowflake save the day?

Read on for a peek at the next book
in the Unicorn Academy series!

CHAPTER 1

"Stay very still," Olivia whispered to Snowflake as they hid behind the marble statue of a flying unicorn.

"Should we go now?" asked Snowflake eagerly. The December air was icy, and Snowflake's breath froze in little clouds as she spoke.

"Not yet," said Olivia, her green eyes on Isabel, who was patrolling in front of the apple tree that the girls were using as base in their game of tag. "We need to wait until Isabel and Cloud get distracted." Her hand flew to her mouth. "Oh no! I think I'm going to . . . *Aaaatishooo!*"

"There they are!" yelled Isabel.

"Go, Snowflake!" shrieked Olivia. Snowflake leaped out from behind the statue, the sunlight making the silver and blue stars on her white coat shine. She charged toward the apple tree, swerving nimbly around Cloud. Olivia's red hair flew out behind her as Snowflake tried her hardest to get

to base, but Scarlett and Blaze, who were also catchers in the game, came galloping up from the

right-hand side. Scarlett's arm was outstretched. Snowflake tried to get past Blaze, but Blaze was one of the fastest unicorns at Unicorn Academy, and Scarlett's hand lightly tagged Olivia's arm.

"Got you!"

Isabel whooped. "Way to go, Scarlett!"

"Sorry, Snowflake," Olivia apologized as they came to a stop.

"It doesn't matter," whinnied Snowflake, shaking her long mane. "It's fun whether we're the catchers or the people hiding!"

Isabel looked around. "Come out! Come out! Wherever you are!" she sang to their three friends, who were still hidden.

Olivia caught a glimpse of a multicolored mane behind a rosebush. "Sophia and Rainbow are over there!" she cried. "Catch them!"

The game continued until all the girls from Sapphire dorm had been caught.

"I need a rest!" said Olivia, fanning her face.

"Me too," said Layla, trotting up on Dancer.

"Play for a little longer, pleeease?" begged Scarlett. "It's our last weekend before the graduation ball. There won't be time to play next week, and then after that we'll all be going home."

The six girls from Sapphire dorm sighed. They had started at Unicorn Academy almost a year ago. In that time, they had all been given their own unicorn to love and bond with, and they'd had loads of exciting adventures together.

"It's going to be so strange not being here any longer," said Ava, looking around wistfully.

"I'll still be here," Olivia pointed out. "Snowflake hasn't discovered her magic yet, and we haven't bonded, so I won't be allowed to graduate."

Bonding was the highest form of friendship. When a person and their unicorn bonded, a

strand of the person's hair turned the same color as the unicorn's mane, showing they were friends for life. From that moment on, it was their duty to help protect Unicorn Island—the beautiful land where they lived. Olivia's friends all had a colorful streak in their hair—Sophia's was multicolored like Rainbow's mane, Ava's was purple, Isabel's was silver and blue, Scarlett's was red and gold, and Layla, who had bonded with Dancer most recently, had an indigo, yellow, and pink streak.

Olivia touched her own red hair, wishing she could have a blue-and-silver streak to match Snowflake's mane. As if sensing her sadness, Snowflake turned and nuzzled her leg. "We'll bond soon," she told Olivia. "There's time before graduation."

"Yes, there's still ten days!" said Sophia. "We'll help you find Snowflake's magic so we can all graduate together."

"We're not leaving you here with horrible Valentina, Delia, and Jacinta," said Scarlett. "They haven't bonded with their unicorns yet either."

Olivia felt a warm tingly feeling rush through her. Her friends were the best, and if anyone could help her, they could! "Thanks. But look, it won't be so bad if I don't graduate with all of you. My little sister, Matilda, is starting in January, so at least I'll know someone."

"You *are* going to graduate," declared Isabel. "And we are all going to meet up regularly. I know we live far away from each other, but we can sleep over at each other's houses. My room is tiny, but it's so warm in my part of the island that we can sleep outside in hammocks."

"My room's small too, but Dad lets me sleep in one of the empty greenhouses when I have a sleepover," said Ava, whose parents ran a plant nursery.

Olivia's stomach squirmed as everyone described their houses and what fun they'd have all squeezing in for sleepovers. She had a secret she still hadn't told her friends, despite knowing them for almost a year. Olivia's home was like a palace, with twelve bedrooms, an indoor swimming pool,

and a tennis court and lake. But although Olivia's parents were rich, they didn't spoil their two daughters. They believed in working hard—they both had jobs, and the girls were expected to help out at home with the cleaning.

Olivia hadn't told the others about her home and family. When she'd first met them, she hadn't wanted to mention it because she didn't want it to sound like she was showing off. Then it had somehow gotten too late to tell them, and she had ended up keeping it a secret. Whenever any of the others asked, she just changed the subject. It had seemed easier that way, but it was going to cause problems if her friends wanted to visit her house.

"What's your place like, Olivia?" asked Isabel curiously. "Where will we sleep when we come to your house?"

Olivia forced herself to laugh. "Let's see if I graduate first. Now I'm going to go back to

the stables. I promised Snowflake I'd practice braiding her mane and tail with rainbow ribbons for the graduation ball, didn't I, Snowflake?"

Snowflake hid her surprise. "That's right," she agreed.

Olivia stroked Snowflake's neck, grateful she'd backed up her lie.

"I'll come with you," offered Layla. "I love braiding Dancer's mane, and you can tell me about your family. I didn't even know you had a little sister." She smiled at her. "I guess I never asked though."

Olivia's tummy twisted. In the last few months, she had become good friends with quiet, clever Layla, but she didn't want to tell her about her family. "Sorry, Layla. But do you mind if I just go back with Snowflake?"

Layla blinked. "Oh. Okay."

"I really want to spend some time with her on

our own. It might help us to bond," said Olivia quickly.

Layla nodded, but Olivia could see the hurt in her eyes, and she felt guilty as she rode away. She didn't say a word to Snowflake. The unicorn waited until they were on their own and then turned her head and gave Olivia a look. "What's the matter?"

"I feel horrible because I just hurt Layla's feelings, but I don't want her asking about my family. Oh, Snowflake, what am I going to do if everyone wants to come to my house next year?"

Snowflake was the only one who knew the truth about Olivia's home life. "Couldn't you just tell them about your parents? I'm sure none of them will treat you any differently."

"But they might!" said Olivia. "Look how much they laugh at Valentina." She pictured snooty Valentina from Emerald dorm. "Her family is

very rich, and everyone hates her."

"That's only because Valentina is spoiled and mean," said Snowflake. "You're not like that at all. You should tell them the truth."

Olivia hesitated. Even if Snowflake was right and her friends didn't judge her, it didn't change the fact that she'd been keeping secrets from them all year. They wouldn't like that at all. No, she couldn't risk it. She couldn't bear it if they decided they didn't like her anymore.

"Let's talk about something else," she muttered.

"But—"

"No!" interrupted Olivia. "And you have to promise me you won't tell anyone."

"Of course I won't," said Snowflake, shocked. "I wouldn't do anything to make you unhappy."

To Olivia's relief she saw they had reached the stables. "Oooh, isn't it lovely and warm in here," she said, leading Snowflake inside. A cart

rumbled past, filled with a bucket of sky berries.
Olivia scooped up a handful and offered them
to Snowflake. "I bet you're hungry after all that
galloping around."

Olivia was sure Snowflake wanted to say more,
but to her relief, her unicorn just sighed and ate
the berries.

"I'll get some ribbons from the storeroom. I'm
going to braid the prettiest rainbow ever in your
mane."

Dropping a kiss on Snowflake's nose, Olivia

hurried away. It was such a relief to know her secret was safe. Snowflake was totally trustworthy and always agreed to do what Olivia wanted. If only Snowflake could find her magic and bond with her in time to graduate with the others. *But,* said a tiny voice in Olivia's head, *if Snowflake doesn't find her magic, then you won't graduate and your friends will never have to find out the truth.*

She frowned, and for the first time began to wonder if she really wanted to graduate with the others after all.

PuRRmaids

Meet your newest feline friends!

PuRRmaids 1
The Scaredy Cat
Sudipta Bardhan-Qua

PuRRmaids 2
The Catfish Club
Sudipta Bardhan-Quallen

#1277

RHCBooks.com RHCB